STORM BOY

WRITTEN AND ILLUSTRATED BY

Paul Owen Lewis

Whitecap Books
Vancouver / Toronto

Whitecap Books
Vancouver / Toronto
Walrus is a division of Whitecap Books Ltd.
www.whitecap.ca

First published by Beyond Words Publishing, Inc., Hillsboro, Oregon.
Second Canadian edition 1998.
Fourth paperback printing, 2008.

Design and composition: Principia Graphica
Color: Exact Imaging

Printed in China

Canadian Cataloguing in Publication Data
Lewis, Paul Owen
     Storm Boy

          ISBN-13: 978-1-55285-268-2   /   ISBN-10: 1-55285-268-7

          1. Killer whale—Folklore. 2. Indians of North America—British
Columbia—Pacific Coast—Folklore. 3. Folklore—British Columbia—Pacific
Coast. I. Title.
E99.H2L48 1998   j398.2'09711'04529536   C97-911033-5

Also by Paul Owen Lewis:

Davy's Dream
Frog Girl
Grasper
P. Bear's New Year's Party

For Kyle and LeAnn

A chief's son
went fishing
alone,

and a terrible storm arose.

He soon found himself
washed ashore
under a strange sky
he had never seen before.
There was a village there.
The houses, the canoes,
and even the people
were very large.

"I am a chief's son,
and I am lost.
A storm has brought me to you,"
said the boy.
"We know this. You are welcome,
son of a chief from above,"
said one who appeared like
a chief himself.
And together they entered
the largest house of all.

Inside, the house was crowded
with finely dressed people
enjoying a feast.
They gave him a blanket to wear
and a fish to eat,
but the fish was not cut up
or cooked.

Strange, too, on the walls all around were what looked like killer whales.

After they finished eating, the chief said to the others, "Let us sing a welcome song and invite our

guest to join in the dance of our people."

"You are welcome! You are welcome! Son of a chief from above!" they sang.

The boy and his hosts began to dance around the fire together to the steady beat of the drums.

He matched them step for step, and the chief smiled when he saw that the boy had so quickly learned their dance.

In return, the boy offered to teach the songs and dances of his own people. The chief was delighted and now followed the boy's lead.

The celebration went on in this way for many long hours, the boy and his new friends each learning from the other.

But though the boy was enjoying himself, he began
to think more and more of home with each song he sang.

He missed his father and mother and wondered if
he would ever find his way back to them again.

Suddenly, the drumming and
dancing stopped.
The chief turned to him and said,
"We are glad that the storm has
brought you to our village,
but now you are thinking
of your own.

"When you wish to return,"
he continued, "grip my staff tightly
and stand behind me.
Close your eyes and
think of your own home,
wishing to be there only."
The boy did as he was told.
He took the staff and
stepped behind the chief.
Closing his eyes,
he pictured his father and
mother, his house, and
the people of his village.

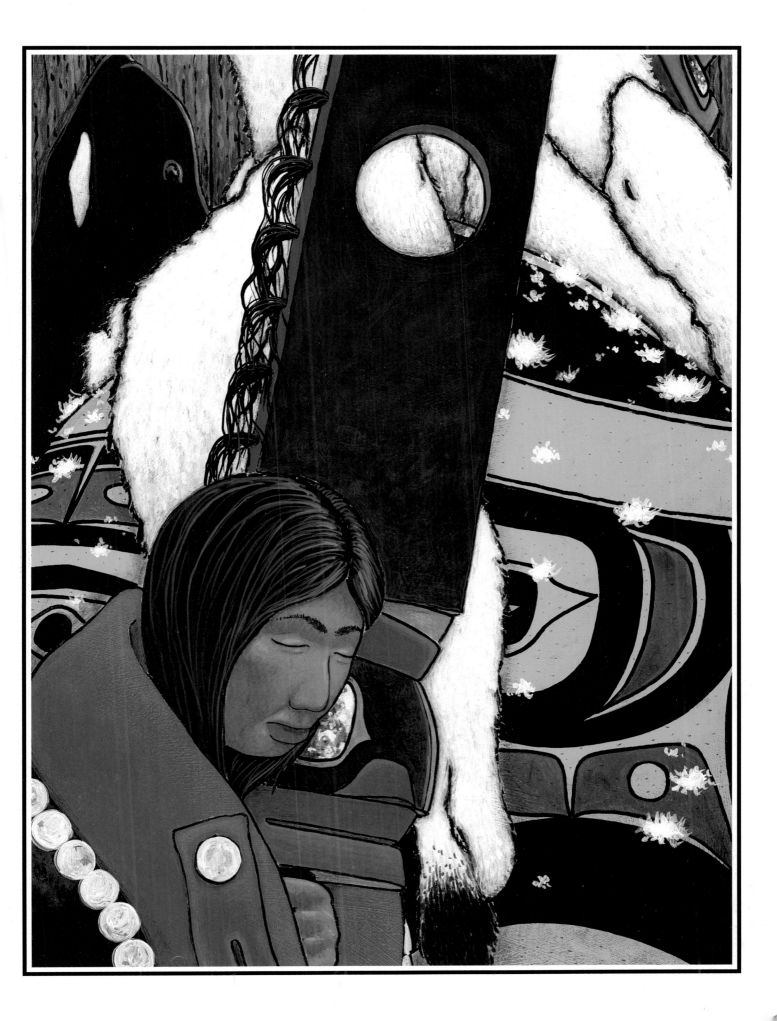

As he did, the boy felt a great surge beneath him,
as if he were being carried upward

at greater and greater speed. He kept his eyes closed
and held on tight.

The motion stopped
and the boy opened his eyes.
There he was, lying on the beach
in front of his very own village!

"My son," cried his mother,
"where have you been? We
thought you were lost in a storm
a year ago!"

"I was lost in a storm—but it
was only yesterday!" exclaimed
the boy.

But a year's time had indeed
passed since he had disappeared
in the storm.
That night the whole village
celebrated his return and
marveled at the boy as he
danced with the staff and told
of the large and mysterious
people under the strange sky.

Author's Note

Common to all the world's mythologies is the Adventure of the Hero, whose pattern of experience renowned scholar Joseph Campbell described in three rites of passage: *separation, initiation, and return.* "A hero ventures forth from the world of common day into a region of supernatural wonder: fabulous forces are there encountered and a decisive victory is won: the hero comes back from this mysterious adventure with the power to bestow boons on his fellow man."[1] In no place is this universal theme more powerfully represented than in the rich oral traditions and bold graphic art of the Haida, Tlingit, and other Native peoples of the Northwest Coast of North America.

This cosmology held that animals possessed spirits or souls identical to human beings and were therefore referred to as *people.* There were wolf people, eagle people, and killer whale people, just as there were human people. "Animals had their own territories, villages, houses, canoes, and chiefs, and many were capable of changing into human form at will, blurring the distinction between animals and humans even more. In their own houses they used human form, and when they wished to appear in their animal form they put on cloaks and masks and spoke their animal language. The myths frequently tell of heroes being escorted by spirit beings through cosmic doorways beyond which lie villages of people who at some stage betray the fact that they are really bear people or salmon people."[2] *Storm Boy* is just such an adventure, reflecting Campbell's three rites of passage with event-motifs unique to Northwest Coast lore.

In an effort to present a degree of authenticity in the telling, a picture-book format has been deliberately chosen in which the text or verbal content is spare and the bulk of the culturally significant detail is communicated by the art. Therefore, for those readers interested in or unfamiliar with Northwest Coast culture and art, I offer the following outline and elaboration:

Northwest Coast motifs of
SEPARATION

• *Wandering too far from the village invites supernatural encounters.*
The boy is out of sight of his village and in bad weather. His identity is indicated by the style of the canoe, which is Haida; by the text, "A chief's son"; and by his clothing—his woven cedar-bark skirt is fur-lined, a sign of wealth. Heroes were most often of high caste or rank. He is a Haida prince.

• *Mysterious entrance to the Spirit World.*
In the presence of killer whales, the boy is thrown from his canoe into the sea, passes through it, and enters into another realm below.

Northwest Coast motifs of
INITIATION

• *Animals encountered in human form.*
The grand scale of the village and the displays of killer whale crest art indicate killer whale people. The frontal pole carving indicates that it is the house of a supernatural killer whale chief—more than one dorsal fin (here there are two) indicates high rank, and the holes through the fins indicate that it is of the supernatural realm. The people are dressed in ceremonial attire, hinting that a high occasion is imminent. The boy claims his high rank as a prince and is formally welcomed by the killer whale chief.

• *Exchange of gifts and culture—"potlatching."*
Inside the house the boy notices natural killer whale forms. These are the "cloaks" that the killer whale people don to appear in the natural world. After receiving gifts of food and a blanket with a killer whale crest, the boy is taught the killer whale's dance—the most valuable of gifts and one befitting his high status. One could even argue that these are signs of his adoption by the killer whales. Dancing around the rising sparks of the cedar-wood fire, the chief punctuates this event by spreading white